SHOW THE WORLD!

WRITTEN BY **Angela Dalton**

ILLUSTRATED BY **Daria Peoples**

VIKING

VIKING
An imprint of Penguin Random House LLC, New York

First published in the United States of America by Viking,
an imprint of Penguin Random House LLC, 2022

Visit us online at penguinrandomhouse.com.

Library of Congress Cataloging-in-Publication Data is available.

Manufactured in the United States of America

ISBN 9780593351390

1 3 5 7 9 10 8 6 4 2

PC

Edited by Liza Kaplan.
Design by Monique Sterling.

Text set in Bugbear.

Artwork created with oil on paper and illustration board.

Map art on endpapers by Marcia Wong

For JDM. My belief in all you can do is endless. Show the world!
—A. D.

For the children of Oakland. Y'all better show them!
—D. P.

Look around. Can you see?
The many spaces, places, and ways to
show the world all that you can be?

What will you do . . .
or say . . .
or make . . .
to express who you are?

A space you fill with sound?
Like a heart-pounding bass . . .

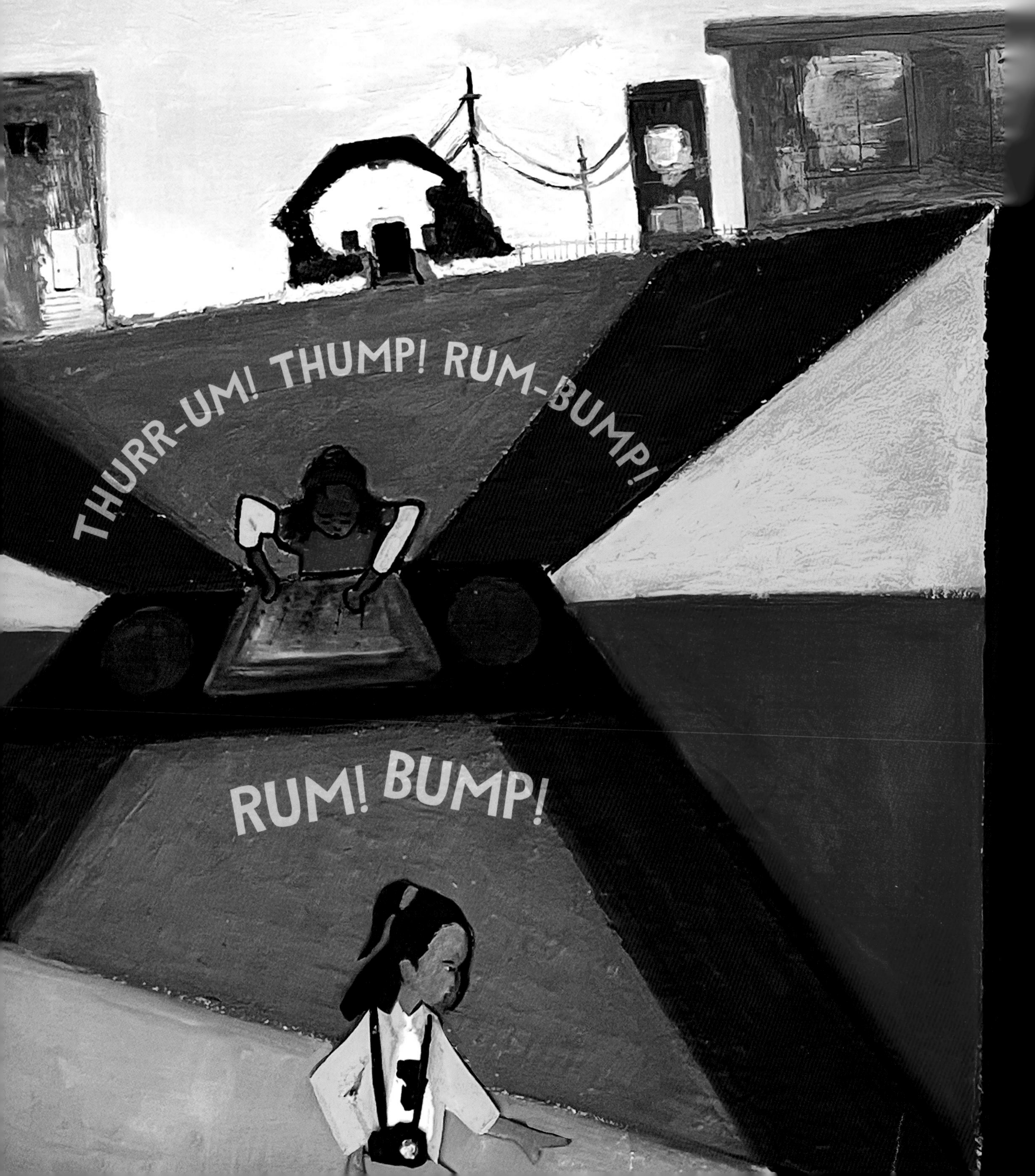

or notes that flutter like hummingbird wings.

Perhaps it's a space that you fill with melody? A shimmering soprano. A smooth alto. Where your words can be sung . . .

or spoken?
How I feel . . . is so real. I need y'all . . . to listen.
Yes, sir!
Say it!
Speak it!
Word!

Maybe *you're* the instrument, telling stories with your own unique dance moves. A twirl, a leap, a glide . . .

Maybe your creative space is blank . . .

patiently waiting for you to fill it with powerful text.

Language that makes you feel something; that makes you think something; that makes you *do* something.

Or perhaps it's a place where your sense of taste can turn everyday ingredients into something extraordinary.

Maybe your voice comes alive through fabric. Your story gathered, formed, stitched, and patterned, a hint of sparkle tucked here and there.

Is your expression captured in a flash?
Images that catch your eye; that you
share with pride and treasure forever?

or collect things found in the world around you.

Is there a place where you shine? A space you fill with all the things that inspire you?

Somewhere you can sit quietly while tiny seeds of ideas swirl around in your head, until one plants itself and begins to grow . . .

and grow. And grow.

Then, one day . . .

TA-DA!
Are you ready to do
or say or create
something?
Do you know
what it will be?
There's no rush.
Take your time.

But when you're ready . . .

SHOW THE
WORLD
ALL THAT
YOU CAN BE!

APR   2022

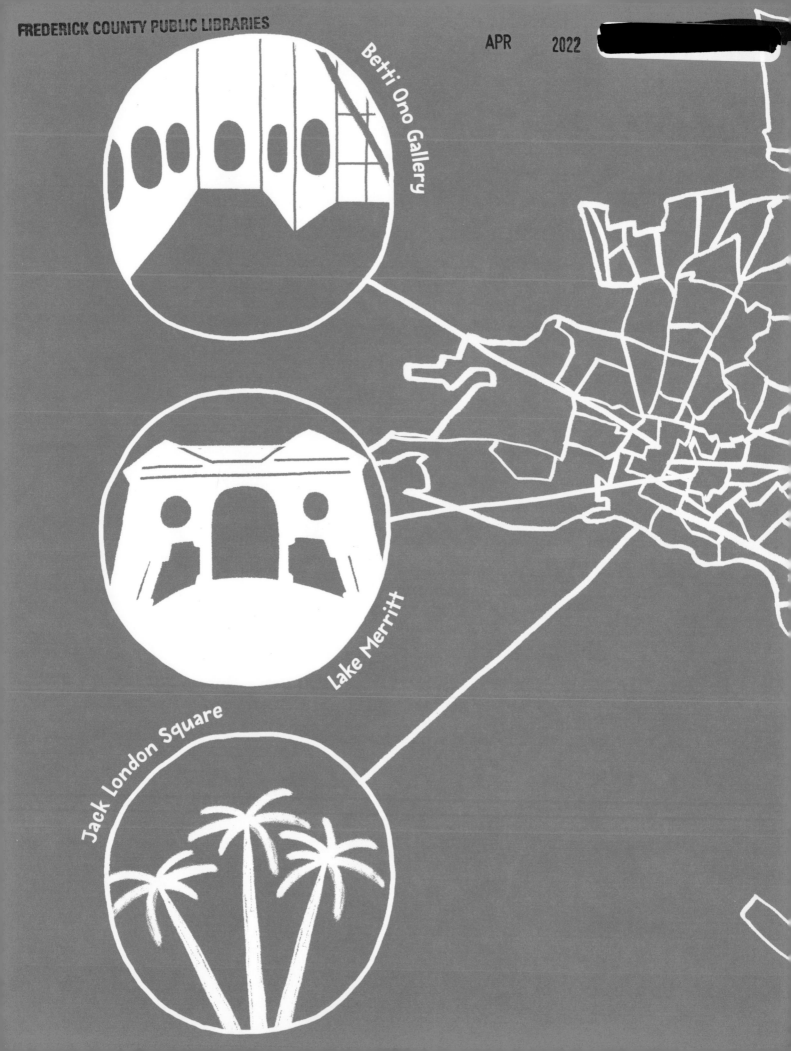

Betti Ono Gallery

Lake Merritt

Jack London Square